WORSE
and
WORSE
on Noah's Ark

by Leslie Kimmelman

Illustrated by Vivian Mineker

APPLES & HONEY PRESS

Great editors can also come in pairs—
a big thank you to Ann and Dena.
— LK

To my father, Sam, the most devoted man I know,
especially to his faith and his family.
— VM

A Note from the Author:

In Judaism, there is a long tradition of *midrash*—elaborating or filling in the gaps to

interpret and more completely understand stories from the Bible. I've written my Noah's

Ark story in that spirit, and taken some creative license in the details of the telling.

Apples & Honey Press
An imprint of Behrman House Publishers
Millburn, New Jersey 07041
www.applesandhoneypress.com

Text copyright © 2020 by Leslie Kimmelman
Illustrations copyright © 2020 by Vivian Mineker

ISBN 978-1-68115-554-8

Library of Congress Cataloging-in-Publication Data
Names: Kimmelman, Leslie, author. | Mineker, Vivian, illustrator.
Title: Worse and worse on Noah's ark / by Leslie Kimmelman ; illustrated by
  Vivian Mineker.
Description: Millburn, New Jersey : Apples & Honey Press, an imprint of
  Behrman House Publishers, [2020] | Summary: Between bad weather, hard
  work, and a food shortage, passengers on Noah's ark wonder if things could
  get worse until, on day thirty-two, Noah helps them to make it all better.
  Includes author's note about empathy.
Identifiers: LCCN 2019016172 | ISBN 9781681155548
Subjects: | CYAC: Noah's ark—Fiction. | Deluge—Fiction. | Animals—Fiction.
  | Empathy—Fiction.
Classification: LCC PZ7.K56493 Wor 2020 | DDC [E]—dc23
LC record available at https://lccn.loc.gov/2019016172

The illustrations for this book were created with watercolor, colored pencils, and digital techniques.

Design by Anne Redmond
Edited by Dena Neusner
Art direction by Ann Koffsky

Printed in China

9 8 7 6 5 4 3 2 1

022130.4K1/B1633/A4

The weather in Noah's neighborhood was terrible.
There were huge dark clouds overhead.
There hadn't been sunshine in weeks.

Noah tried to keep sunshiny inside.
"All in God's good time," he reminded himself.

Then he heard from God personally.

"Noah, build an ark," God said.
"Build the most enormous ark you can."

It seemed like an odd request, but when God spoke,
Noah listened. So he built a gigantic ark.

Noah's whole family helped. They worked side by side from morning till night.

"This ark is way too big for us," said Mrs. Noah. "Why does it have to be so huge?"

"Because God said so," Noah answered.

"*Meshuggah*," Mrs. Noah mumbled, stopping to rest for a moment. "Just plain foolish. Could things get any worse?"

THINGS GOT WORSE.

The skies opened up.
It rained all day . . .
   and the next day . . .
      and then the next.

Noah kept building. His sons were wet and grumpy.
"Oy, could things get any worse?" they complained.

THINGS GOT WORSE.

It rained all *week* . . .
and then the next week.

WORSE, and **WORSE**, and **WORSE**.

When the ark was finally finished, Noah
invited some friends aboard, two by two.
Soon there wasn't an inch of space to spare.

"Welcome!" said Noah.

"Wipe your feet, please!" begged Mrs. Noah,
"and be careful with the claws."
She swept up behind them.
"Oy vey, what a day," she fussed.
"Could things get any worse?"

THINGS GOT WORSE.

Before long, the ark was alone, tossed on an endless ocean.
Still, the rain came down,

and down,

and down.

On day five, the animals got seasick.

"Feh!" Noah's sons exclaimed, fetching mops and buckets.
"Could things get any worse?"

THINGS GOT WORSE.

On day twelve, the scarlet macaws and the peacocks made fun of the zebras and penguins, who were only black and white.

"We're all God's creatures," Noah reminded them. "We're all equally beautiful in God's eyes."

The lions and howler
monkeys argued about
who was loudest.
"Enough!" said Noah.

The sloths slept
through everything.

But Noah's family did not.
"COULD THINGS GET ANY WORSE?"
they yelled over the commotion.

THINGS GOT WORSE.

On the twenty-first day, an armadillo broke its shell,
sliding from one side of the ark to the other.

And on day twenty-nine, the skunks, terrified by
thunder and lightning, made quite a stink.

"Pee-yew," grumbled Noah's sons.
"Could things get any worse?" asked their wives.

THINGS GOT WORSE.

Food was running low.
The grizzly bears licked their lips when
the antelopes crossed their path. . . .

The owls looked longingly at the mice.

"Worse and worse," kvetched Mrs. Noah,
looking in the pantry for something—
anything—to feed the passengers.

On day thirty-two, the ark sprang a leak.
Water came in an inch at a time.

The squirrels sneezed.
The shrews shivered.
The kangaroos coughed.
Everyone was shouting.

What a hullabaloo! What a **DISASTER**!

"Here's a thought,"
said Noah calmly.
"What if we work together
to fix the leak?"

Everyone stopped and stared.
"That may be worth trying,"
Mrs. Noah finally said.

One of the rhinos plugged up the hole with his horn.

Meanwhile, the horses and cows fetched hay,
and the pigs brought mud.

Mrs. Noah mixed everything together.
The tigers patted the concoction into the hole
with their huge paws.
The elephants vacuumed up the water.

Before long, the ark was dry once more.
"Good job, all," said Noah quietly.

Then something surprising happened.
Life on the ark began to change.

It was still cramped and messy,
and the weather was still terrible,
but no one minded as much.
They were looking after one another.

When cabin fever broke out,
the aardvarks organized a party.
Everybody helped.

When an especially large wave slammed the vessel,
the animals tended to one another's bumps and bruises.

There was so much harmony on board that Mrs. Noah started a choir!
Some nearby humpback whales joined in.

After forty days, the rains s-l-o-w-e-d . . . and then stopped.

One afternoon the ark finally came to a stop on the tip-top of Mount Ararat. Noah sent out a dove to search for dry land. But the bird soon returned.

There was nothing but water everywhere.

"Just wait," Noah reassured the disappointed animals. "Things are bound to get better."

Noah sent out the dove again.
This time it did not return. It had found dry land.

"At last!" exclaimed Mrs. Noah, smiling.
She opened the doors wide, and the animals left the ark as they had
entered, two by two—leaping, running, bouncing, scampering, flying.
Noah and Mrs. Noah and their family followed.

The air outside was cool and fresh.
The land was green and lush.
The flood was over.

"Could things get any better?"
they asked, barked, roared, honked,
purred, clucked, and chirped.

THINGS GOT BETTER!

A Note from the Author

It's not easy to get along when you're crowded
together on an ark . . . or at home.
How can creatures live together in harmony?
Try putting yourself in someone else's
shoes—or paws! That's called empathy.
Do you think it's easier to get along if you
understand how the other person feels?
How can you live peacefully with others in
your family? With friends?

Wishing you rainbows,
Leslie